MW00479152

ON THE ROAD TO LOVE SERIES

USA TODAY BESTSELLING AUTHOR

Verlene Landon

COPYRIGHT

Dangerous Curve Ahead
previously titled *Unexpected Hero*
Copyright © 2019 Verlene Landon - Rusty Halo Books
All rights reserved.

Cover Design: Bookend Designs
Editing: My Brother's Editor

This book is a work of fiction. People, places, events, and situations are the product of the author's imagination. Any resemblance to actual persons, living, dead, undead, immortal, or living in a douche-like state, or historical events, is purely coincidental.

ISBN: 978-1736502327

To anyone who's had sex in a functional garage on a sturdy workbench and ended up with axle grease on their ass.

CHAPTER 1

*I should've fucking known better, but I was young and in love —
dangerous combination.*

*It took years to realize I wouldn't get away from him until I
was dead.*

*So, that's why I'm sitting here dressed like a ninety-year-old
woman with a bad back and hard of hearing at my own damn
funeral.*

*I don't recommend it, by the way, attending your own funeral.
It's just a bunch of folks who didn't give two shits about you while
you were alive, blubbering on about what a great person you were.
What a hole you left in their life, and they don't know how they
can ever fill it.*

*Um, I know, Janice, you'll fill it with the sympathy you milk
from my death, losing one of your 'closest' friends. One you loved so*

fucking much you didn't check on in the hospital, or text hello to, or ask about all the bruises and broken bones or why you couldn't see her, sometimes for a few months.

Yes, Janice, you'll glut on the drama of "losing your dear friend," and roll around like the flea covered bitch you are in the spotlight.

Rachel never expected to be bitter by thirty, but there she was killing it. She also never expected to be running from a man she'd given her body and soul to . . . again, killing it.

The over-combed pastor, of a church she'd never been to, spoke the final prayer for her dear sweet soul. When he invited folks up to pay their last respects to a closed casket since she'd been *cremated*, Rachel decided that was her cue. She rose slowly with a lot of groaning and shuffled geriatrically out the door.

Once outside, she almost straightened herself upright to take a deep breath, but thankfully a passing car reminded her that Tony could be watching. She knew he had eyes everywhere and was stunned he hadn't been at the service. Not stunned, she reminded herself. He had his private service over the urn he took home and probably used as an ashtray, *just like when I was alive.*

Tony wasn't the type to stand elbow to elbow with the mere common folk. She had to mask her giggle as she strolled down the stairs and started her agonizingly slow walk to the home she "resided" in.

Tony wasn't as mobbed up as he pretended to be. Hell, he wasn't even Italian, he was from some Podunk town in Kentucky. He had rewritten his history, as did his dad. It took almost ten years for her to ferret out that much.

That was the only thing she could ever even remotely thank him for. Finding out how he'd rewritten his history helped her rewrite her future.

His *mob family* consisted of his half-brother, two uncles, a cousin, and a few outsiders he brought in as muscle. Even with such a pathetic mob family, he managed to keep his little corner of the county on lock. Everyone was terrified of him, and if Rachel were to be honest with herself, that was part of the appeal that led her into the mess in the first place.

His dark asshole personality drew her nineteen-year-old self with an inexplicable force. Tony was the sexy bad boy she thought she could tame but not completely squash what attracted her.

Women loved their fucking bad boys, that's for sure. *Until they got an honest to goodness* bad *one.*

She wasn't talking about the type you find in romance novels with the gritty appealing attitude that hides the heart of a poet type. No, Tony was the type she wouldn't wish on her worst enemy, the rough exterior that masked the heart of a sociopath type.

Rachel had been so lost in her thoughts; she'd let her guard slip. It wasn't until a movement across the street caught her attention that she realized how much she'd exposed herself.

Usually, she'd shuffle into the home she "lived" in, pop into her room for a few, then slink out the back. Her real place was just across the alley. Nothing grand, a small loft over a garage that thankfully was closed down due to a family death.

Not that death should ever be celebrated, but it did help her maintain her cover. Having rented it just days before Jimmy's untimely demise had been a blessing. No one even knew she was there except the family who couldn't do much until the estate was settled or her lease was up, whichever came first.

Thank God I plotted my getaway months beforehand. Sneaking away in Eunice Duncan's persona whenever Tony was preoccupied turned out to be crucial for her ultimate escape, almost more so than Tabitha.

She'd established Eunice, no middle name, Duncan and Tabitha Lynn Caldwell long before Rachel Louisa Miller bought the farm.

With the suspicious car across the street, Rachel would have to improvise and alter her routine.

Eunice halted her shuffle and looked up at her building, confused. Turning in an agonizingly slow circle, she surveyed her surroundings as if seeing them for the first time, then turned back to the building. With a confident nod, she used the handrail and her cane to assist her ascent.

Rachel struggled with the heavy door the way Eunice always did, and with plenty of noise. Predictably, one of the staff came to her aid.

"That door still giving you fits, Ms. Duncan?" Annabelle asked as she opened the door.

Rachel shouted back, "What was that, dear?"

One lesson Tony taught her well was predictability can mean your death or your survival, depending on how you wield it.

In Annabelle's case, Rachel wielded her as survival. "I SAID, THIS OLD DOOR IS STILL GIVING YOU FITS. I NEED TO CALL MAINTENANCE."

As the door slowly closed behind them, Rachel caught the slightest glimpse of the car . . . and the man leaning against the hood.

Her blood ran cold as what her eyes beheld relayed that information to her brain. It was Vin, Tony's brother, an enforcer.

As Annabelle helped her to her room, her mind was reeling. If he was here, did that mean Tony knew? No, that was impossible. Tony would have been with him if his suspicions were strong enough.

Once in her room, she locked the door, tossed her cane, and began the exhausting process of analyzing everything out loud.

"Think, Rach, think. If Tony had more than just suspicions of the possibility I hadn't died, he would have shown himself. Yes, he would bring backup because he's a pussy, but he would want to savor the look on my face when he busted me."

The wig was next to go before she realized she needed to be somewhat ready to answer the door. Rachel raced to the bathroom and secured the wig again . . . poorly as Eunice was known to do.

She'd decided early on that it would make more sense for an old lady to have an apparent full wig to cover up her naturally thinning hair than it would to try to add a thinning wig and make it look real.

Looking at herself in the mirror gave her pause. Her cloudy contacts hid her striking green eyes well. Even she couldn't tell they weren't the peepers of an old woman.

The wrinkles looked authentic enough to make her shudder. She'd practically shaved her head underneath and dyed it gray in case she ever lost her wig in public.

Something about the old face looking back at her brought some calm. There was no way anyone could recognize her unless they took her clothes off. She couldn't hide how fit she was, although she was damn sure trying.

Calmly, she puzzled out Vin's appearance. He was checking out everyone at the service she'd bet. Trying to find out whom she would've known or spent time with who wasn't in Tony's circle. Vin's appearance is for the strict purpose of seeing if I told anyone anything and how much.

Rachel calmed herself down with that realization. She expected this; she'd even left the Eunice trail so he wouldn't look for Rachel here. It was where the trail goes cold or abruptly ends that he would search the hardest, so she led it to her service on purpose.

This was an expected threat assessment, plain and simple. Why he sent Vin was what scared her. If he were here, he would assess and resolve. Meaning if a threat was found, he'd make sure they couldn't harm his brother ever again. That was Vin's specialty.

Rachel had firsthand knowledge of how he operated, and she knew to steer clear. That, however, wasn't going to be a possibility. She was positive he would want to talk to Eunice, even at her advanced age, if she was a loose end . . . a threat, she'd need to be tied up same as any.

A quick peek through the blinds told her Vin had moved on . . . for now. Probably checking out everyone else who'd attended the service. Mentally preparing herself for a meeting that would inevitably happen in a few days, Rachel shed Eunice and stepped through the back door as Tabitha.

CHAPTER 2

Old lady patrol wasn't Vin's idea of a decent use of his time. He'd have to circle back and chat her up and see what she knew or could even remember.

Tony was insane if he thought some hunched over old biddy was a threat to him. Still, he'd sweet talk the staff and learn what he could about her then come back to feel her out.

The small handful of others at Rachel's service were pretty much cleared, considering Tony was sleeping with the one who'd be most likely to have info made his job considerably easier.

Flicking his cigarette butt into the street, Vin rounded the hood then drove down the block. He decided to walk back to the Helping Hands Independent

Living. That's just a fancy way of saying subsidized apartments for old folks whose family can't afford a nursing facility. Although the likelihood that anyone noticed him at all was nil, he was cautious by nature.

Vin damn near snatched the door off the hinges. The same door old Eunice couldn't budge. *Yeah, Tony, she's a real threat, that one.* Even if Rachel had spilled her guts to the lady, which he highly doubted, she probably couldn't even remember whose service she'd just attended. Hell, she'd looked so fucking lost just trying to get home.

Wiping all thoughts of Rachel and Tony from his mind, Vin went into seduction mode.

As her nametag proclaimed, Annabelle's eyes went wide as she drank him in. A reaction he was used to. Not that he was conceited, but he knew most women liked the way he looked, and he wasn't above using it to his advantage.

He'd learned early on his dark eyes and bald head was pretty much a thigh spreader.

Just flirt with the lady, get the information and go. Vin was over this whole obsession Tony had with Rachel. He was over the whole Rachel thing in general. She was dead, and that was that. It didn't matter if some people wished she wasn't, wishing didn't change shit. Vin was living proof of that. If wishes mattered, he wouldn't be working for his demented brother, he wouldn't be evaluating a geriatric threat, and he wouldn't be seeing a ghost while rummaging through what-ifs in his sleep.

Rachel was taking up way too much space in his life and head, just as she had when she'd been alive for fuck's sake.

"Well, hello handsome, which one of our lucky residents are you here to visit today?"

Her voice was laced with syrupy sweet seduction that did absolutely nothing for him. She was so not his type, not that his type would even be able to tempt him right now anyway. Erasing all traces of deception from his face, Vin turned up the charm.

Leaning against the desk, he met Annabelle's gaze and took note of when her pupils dilated, and her tongue darted out to wet her lips. It was an unconscious move most women made, and they weren't even aware of it. The whole *notice me, I want to kiss you,* look.

"Well hello to you too, beautiful. I hope your day is as bright as that smile is." *Laying it on a bit thick, Vin. You might want to scale it back before she climbs the desk and offers up the pussy on a platter.*

Annabelle practically squirted on the floor when he dropped the hand he was leaning on the counter with to gently stroke her hand. Just once and he pulled back. He could see the moment as if it were a flashing neon sign saying she would give him any information he wanted, even if it were against policy. And she would do it all for the illusion that he might stick his dick in her in some capacity.

"I wanted to ask about a resident of yours, Eunice Duncan? I am hoping you could tell me a bit about her." A flash of scrutiny ran across her face, but a crooked smile from him chased it away.

A sigh preceded her seemingly melted posture. "Eunice? Sweet old lady, no family to speak of." To go the extra mile, Annabelle reached for a file and flipped through it. "She signed on with us months ago; however, she didn't become a regular fixture until a few days ago. Before that, we saw her once in a blue moon."

She was still droning on, but Vin was processing the info she'd just given him. The likelihood Rachel even spoke to her was negligible, but something about Eunice puzzled him a bit.

Why have an apartment and not stay, especially at her age. It wouldn't be likely she would be able to maintain two places. And what was her connection to Rachel? He knew everything there was to know about Rachel, hell, he knew more than Tony.

Half the things Tony had sent him to find out before they were "a thing" and after, he never shared. Things Tony didn't need to know. Like how Rachel had been a fantastic sculptor or how the first asshole she'd ever slept with only did it to brag to his buddies, complete with photographic proof.

The assault beef I caught for that one had been worth it, even though no one else knew it wasn't a random drunken bar brawl. He'd been stone-cold sober.

At this point, he deemed Eunice a total non-threat so that he could walk away having done his due diligence for Tony, but he stood there anyway, listening to what Annabelle had to say. Rachel meant something to Eunice or the other way around, and he wanted to know how and why.

When Annabelle closed the file, Vin gifted her a panty-melting smile as if he had been hanging on every word. "Thank you so much, Annabelle, you've been most helpful." Vin allowed his eyes to drift down the hall, communicating his intention. "I'd like to visit Eunice, is her apartment this way?"

Vin turned back toward the lady who was gooey-eyed over him. His gaze caught on a rusty-colored object on a decorative table. Sitting there in the sparse lobby off to the left he'd almost overlooked. Lobby was a gross overstatement; it was two chairs and a table in an alcove.

Without thought, he was pulled toward the abstract piece of art that looked like an exploding sun and a blooming flower at the same time.

His scarred fingers reached out to trace the lines of the baked clay. He recognized the style, although he hadn't seen it in ten years. There was no mistaking who created it. *Rachel.*

"Where did you come by this?" His question was harshly shot from his mouth and sent Annabelle recoiling. *Damn it. Calm the fuck down.*

What struck him most was he not only knew the style; he knew the exact piece. Letting his hands drift to the backside under a ray slash petal, he confirmed that knowledge with the crack that ran horizontally before making a sharp turn north.

It was one of the many things Tony had ordered him to destroy, along with everything else Rachel owned before Tony owned her. To Tony, Rachel's things were all just possessions to be tossed away. Rachel didn't know it, hell, no one did, but he'd convinced Tony he would have more leverage if he put her stuff in storage instead. *An act of love toward his new lady,* he'd told him. *"Plus, if they mean anything to her, you can threaten to destroy them as needed."*

His brother had praised his genius.

It worked too, Rachel was grateful to Tony for storing her stuff, and he got stuck with shuttling her back and forth to the storage facility whenever the mood struck her, and Tony allowed.

That was in the beginning when she still had hope. Toward the end, she had nothing, he and Tony had seen to that. Her spirit was broken, and she… which brought him back to the present. Why the fuck did Tony send him on this ridiculous mission? Any rebellion Rachel had was beaten out of her long before the accident.

The sculpture taunted him, accusing him of helping snuff out her fire long before he'd played a role in snuffing out her life. Maybe her accident was no accident at all. *Could Rachel have taken her own life to get away from Tony?* It sure seemed that way; she had given away her first sculpture, the one that started her love of molding clay.

The possibility made him want to vomit. *Why couldn't you just hold—*

"Ms. Eunice placed it there. Said her friend made it, and she thought the area could use a little art. I didn't have the heart to tell her no, it seemed to make her so happy, so I left it there."

Annabelle's voice halted the rise of bile. "This friend, was her name Rachel?" He couldn't keep the emotion from his voice.

"Was? Oh, the memorial service, so sad. You must've known her? We never had the pleasure here, but she sure meant a lot to Ms. Duncan."

"Yes, I knew her, but the sculpture?" No matter how hard he tried, Vin couldn't keep the impatience out of his voice.

"I'm not sure, but I don't think it was Rachel who made it or if Eunice even remembers who did. She seemed lost when I asked her. The person who might know though is Tabitha."

"Tabitha?"

"Yeah, Tabitha, or Tabby as Eunice calls her. She must live close by; she visits Eunice every so often. Ms. Duncan is supposed to register visitors, for the safety of all the residents, but we let it slide." Annabelle leaned in and whispered the next words like they were a secret.

"We think she must be terminal, cancer or something, shaved head and rather small. Anyway, we never see her arrive, and she sneaks out quiet as a church mouse. Never any trouble and she must live close by because she always leaves through the back and no car or bicycle or…"

Vin didn't hear another word. Instead, he raced out the front door and hoofed it around back. If this Tabitha has any connection to Rachel, he needed to know, especially if she was sick. Maybe the chance to make amends didn't die with Rachel.

His heartbeat for what felt like the first time in six days.

CHAPTER 3

Rachel needed to decompress after seeing Vin. The sight of that man threw her off-balance and filled her with more self-hate than the sight of Tony at this point in her life.

She paced the garage to clear her head. It wasn't working. Instead of continuing to wear down the concrete, she began gathering her supplies. For each one she set on the table, she allowed herself to evaluate a bit of the past. She hoped to give it its due, then she could let it flow from her to clay and be gone.

Tony was a youthful mistake that she let get out of hand. She'd been weak and should've left the first time he backhanded her, but opted to stay. It only got worse when she arrived at her new home and Tony threw her in the deep end, so to speak. A pattern developed and he got crueler, and she just took it. There was no explanation for it other than she'd needed to come into her own and she finally did.

So while Tony was the dick who'd abused her and tried to break her... hell, *did* break her, she was the mouse who allowed it. That was one part she might never get over.

Ahhhhh, she screamed in her head as she molded the clay.

Why am I so fucking stupid? For an entire decade, I allowed him to tear me down.

It was only when she decided she deserved more, did things start to change for her; she made them change...*she'd changed.*

Vin was a different story. *Another story of self-hate that will follow me to my grave...my real one.*

She knew exactly who the fuck he was, unlike Tony, who'd blindsided her with his charm and classic good looks. At nineteen, everything Tony was and had, impressed her, and she went in ignorant to what lurked beneath that designer suit.

No, Vin was different. She knew who and what he was from the get-go, he was transparent as fuck from day one. Vin even looked the part of the bad guy. Dark and scarred. His eyes were empty black holes. That wasn't exactly accurate. There were epic storms swirling in those dark depths most days.

Even with all the things she knew to be true about Vin, they had shared…tender wasn't the right word, but moments that weren't steeped in violence.

Like when Tony wasn't anywhere to be found, they played poker for pretzel sticks and gummy bears. On very rare occasions, they broke out that old guitar video game. Vin had an amazing voice, but she was probably the only person on the planet who knew that. In those moments, it was like they were just two friends hanging out because they enjoyed each other's company.

It was the times like that which confused her the most. Just like in the movies, Vin was all hard angles and wore black from head to toe. He made it easy for unsuspecting bystanders to know what he was and step away before he had to show them. Not that she hadn't seen it plenty enough, but she'd glimpsed a softer side too.

Tony, on the other hand, picked his suits by season and had kind eyes if you didn't look too deep. He disarmed folks with a megawatt smile, and they assumed he was a good guy.

Little did they know looks can be deceiving.

There was a weird dynamic between Vin and Tony that Rachel could never puzzle out, and God knew she tried. The first half of her sentence—as she called it—she thought if she could flush it out, she might be able to use it to her advantage.

In hindsight, she'd realized she would've had a better shot of getting it out of Tony than Vin. Vin was more closed off than Tony. Even with the glimpses she'd gotten into a different side of him, no one was allowed in.

Another case of me following the wrong path.

Their sibling relationship felt almost like Vin thought he owed Tony something, so he did his dirty work and all too well at that.

Maybe Tony had some deep-seated childhood trauma at the hands of Vin, or maybe his mom liked Vin better and he took issue with it, who knew. Tony tended to get bent out of shape over non-existent slights or because it was Tuesday.

Now that she was *dead*, she seemed to do her best thinking and self-evaluating. Rachel had to admit that some sick, twisted part of her still found Vin attractive. Like she hadn't learned her lesson enough over the years about that type of bad boy. *They're never worth the piece of your soul it costs you. You can't tame them or fix them.*

Sadly, Vin was, in some warped way, her only friend but also her jailer. He was the one who cleaned her wounds with a click of his tongue and a… *"Why do you bait him, Little One? You know where it always ends."*

Those words never failed to send chills down her spine, not just because of the truth they held. But also pooled warmth in places that shouldn't be warmed by such a violent man.

Maybe I'm just so fucked up I like the violence at this point in life. Rachel couldn't believe that after she fought so hard to be away from it. Also, the thought of Tony or any other man for that reason made her nauseous.

Even with all she knew to be fact about Vin; somehow she was still attracted to him on a level she couldn't control, couldn't explain, and couldn't even rationalize. Maybe it was his not-so-good poker face when gummy bears were on the line or his mad *guitar* skills.

Finally, she quit trying. She chalked it up to some bastardized version of Stockholm syndrome. As much as she feared him, she was also grateful. *I never really feared-feared him, not like I did Tony. Why is that?*

All the nights Tony sent her to Vin's room because he didn't want to look at her, but he refused to leave her unguarded. Vin never once touched her inappropriately, of course, that may have been the threats from Tony rather than any respect or chivalry on his part.

Rachel didn't like to dwell on that shit too long. It put her in a place mentally she was fighting to get out of. Regardless, it was his "friendship" that gave her the strength to make it out and that would always mean something to her. Accepting that would never be easy, but she knew it to be true.

That doesn't mean I ever want to see his face again.

Rachel had to wait it out, and when Vin was done with whatever investigation Tony deemed prudent, they'd move on from her. Then and only then could she "kill" Eunice and even Tabby and leave the area and never look back.

Rachel finally stripped down to her underwear and started kneading the clay. Letting all her thoughts flow from her brain, down her arms, and out of her fingertips. It was only then she began to relax. Tony, Vin, and the last ten years faded away like the tide going out to sea.

She loved being one with the clay. It was almost a sensual experience. She was in that perfect space where she *was* her art. Before she even noticed what happened, she had completed a piece in record time.

Deciding she'd leave it to air dry in the less than ideal environment of the garage bay, she turned. Before she made it to the door, she halted and spun back to the clay.

Really seeing it, her chest constricted. *Fuck me.* For the first time in her life, she thought of destroying her art . . . her very heart. Fist raised and primed to punch it down, she faltered. Art was raw, art was real, and destroying it would never change the part of the artist that resided within it. Still, she couldn't look at it right now, maybe never. Turning it to face the wall, Rachel headed up to tuck into her tiny tub and rinse off the clay that seemed to get everywhere and the spirit gum residue leftover from Eunice.

She'd soaked so long, the water was cooling, and her skin was shriveling, but Rachel hesitated to rise. Baths were one thing she'd always enjoyed, and one luxury she was denied for a long time. Tony thought it was disgusting to soak in your own stew as he called it, so he banned baths. Even had no tubs in his sprawling estate.

Exhaustion was deepening her relaxation when a noise put her on high alert.

Someone's in the garage.

CHAPTER 4

Luck was on his side for once. While searching the area, he'd caught movement in a window above the abandoned garage. The chick he saw through the dirty glass fit the bill of who he was looking for, so he thought to pop the lock and have a look around downstairs.

If he were wrong, he'd be out of there before the person upstairs even had a clue he'd been there.

Picking the old lock to Jimmy's Auto Repair was child's play. Vin just hoped the sickly Tabby was alone up there. He didn't want to deal with Jimmy or anyone else who might be there tonight besides an underweight slip of a sick girl.

This was a recon mission only and not exactly one for Tony, he had to admit. Tony would be satisfied that the only connection to Rachel had one foot in the grave and the other on a banana peel.

Tabby was of no interest to Tony since she hadn't attended the service. He hadn't survived all these years by volunteering information. Vin's was a world of exacts. Follow orders to the letter; no more, no less. Do what needs to be done and live to see another day as a free man.

Free my fucking ass.

He was a prisoner, as much as Rachel had been, only the bars that held him were in his mind and his past. Hers had been both physical and mental, and he would never forgive himself for the part he'd played in that.

But maybe, just maybe, he could try to make amends for at least a microscopic sampling of his sins with Eunice, or this Tabby if she meant something to Rachel.

The dim light filtering in through the breaks in the paper someone had used to block out the sun was enough for him to navigate his way around the racks and tool chests.

The dust motes floating around him seemed to carry the all-too-familiar scent of lavender and dryer sheets. He shook his head in an attempt to cleanse the past from his nostrils.

Rachel had been on his mind so much he was fucking smelling her. His confusion only deepened when his eyes fell to the corner. Tucked away from the tools and remnants of auto parts, were the instruments of a sculptor.

As if drawn by an unseen force, he quietly made his way toward yet more things to bring Rachel back to the front of his mind. *Damn it, I just want to find this sick chick, offer her help and move the fuck on with my life.*

What he saw next added layer to his earlier confusion that he didn't know if he could ever puzzle out.

Sitting among the knives and probes, was a fresh lump of clay, formed into the likeness of an . . . eye?

Reaching for the wooden base that held it, he spun it around. The shape of the eye struck him as familiar, but the destruction it held was foreign. Somehow the artist had captured so much pain inside the widened pupil of the plain clay. No color to give contrast but Vin was mesmerized by the depths that one familiar eye held.

The clay was tacky and he hated that he had marred it with a partial print but he couldn't stop himself from reaching out and trying to wipe away a three-dimensional tear.

At that moment he knew he had to help Tabitha and keep her off of Tony's radar. She had meant something to Rachel, something significant enough for her to have taught her to sculpt with the same feel and emotion she'd once done.

Vin's mind was reeling as to when and how. Sure, Rachel enjoyed a small measure of freedom when Tony was gone, and he was gone a lot, but how had Vin missed it?

To teach someone to sculpt like that would take countless hours and Vin could account for enough of Rachel's time to make that impossible.

Either way, Vin's heart soared at the realization that he could maybe make things a little right with Tabitha. It also broke because the talent and light Rachel had brought to the world, *his* world, was gone and it was all his fault.

Of all the death and mayhem he'd caused, would cause, Rachel's was one he couldn't seem to reconcile.

Every life he'd ended had deserved it. Not Rachel. She'd been innocent of the kind of evil that warranted death, even by Tony's twisted standard.

Vin refocused when he heard a splash of water upstairs. He was not some sentimental chump, he had a wrong to make amends for and he'd found his way to do that. It was upstairs. He'd foot the bill for the best treatment money could buy for whatever fucked up disease she had and clear that death from his soul. So he could move on with his so-called life.

As he crept up the stairs, he found it ironic that he was cleansing one death from his soul so he could cause another and keep his black soul in enough balance he could justify his deeds when he closed his eyes at night.

The door to the offices, which had been converted into a decent sized apartment, was even easier to pop than the main entrance. A slight creak of the hinges broke the relative silence of the space as Vin made his way inside.

No lights were on in the main area of the apartment, but some seeped in under the door he assumed was the bathroom and some moonlight filtered in from a fire escape's open window.

The apartment smelled even more like Rachel than the garage had. Guilt was causing him to lose his shit. *Focus, damn it.*

"Shit," he cursed when a black cat appeared in that window meowing. Choosing to ignore the unexpected distraction, Vin studied the strip of light under the door for signs of motion.

No shadows interrupted the thin bar, so he advanced. For the first time in a long time, he was operating with no plan, just walking in blind.

His next step damn near sent him to the ground. Somehow he managed to bite back a curse and keep from kicking the blasted creature responsible right back out the window where he entered.

"Shoo, shoo." Keeping his voice low wasn't easy since the damned thing was Velcroed to his leg. Doing a figure eight wasn't enough for the devil, no. When Vin bent to remove him from the immediate area gently, the cursed cat wrapped all four paws around his leg and meowed up at him with sad eyes.

Vin was at a complete loss. Animals usually steered clear of him, that whole sense a predator thing. This fucking thing didn't have the sense to know he wanted to throw it through the wall.

Finally, with a little blood and a lot of protest, Vin managed to peel the cat from his shin. Lifting it to his face, he realized it wasn't near as big as it had seemed when it was backlit by the moon. The thing looked like it had a bad case of worms, fleas, and probably the mange.

Its fur wasn't silky, its eyes were weepy, and he was missing an ear. It was the ugliest fucking cat he'd ever seen. While he debated what to do with it, the damned thing licked his nose *and gave a less than enthusiastic meow.*

What the fuck do I know about cats, tossing his shaved head back and forth searching for an answer, Vin's dark eyes landed on the chest in front of a chair.

"You don't have a single survival instinct, do you, little fucker?" The question was rhetorical, but the cat answered anyway as Vin lowered him into the chest and closed the lid.

He wasn't a complete monster, he left it cracked so the thing could breathe and made a mental note to tell Tabitha to let him out.

One immediate problem dealt with, Vin had lost patience, and strode to the bathroom with little finesse and threw open the door.

A full tub of still water greeted him, but no Tabitha. A prickle of warning ran up his spine. As he turned to see what had caused it, something crashed down on his temple. The blow blurred his vision and sent him to the cracked tile.

The last vision he saw was a slim figure looming over him.

"Tabitha?" he breathed before his wonky vision focused on her eyes. Eyes that'd haunted his days and his nights. The spring green color that had fueled every spank session he'd had in the last decade.

The eyes of a dead woman. A dead woman who was smaller and balder than before but a dead one all the same.

Impossible.

"Rachel?" The name left his lips as barely a whisper before unconsciousness claimed him.

CHAPTER 5

"Oh my god, oh my god, oh my god. What have I done?" Rachel panicked as she tied Vin to the bathroom radiator. She hadn't meant to hit him. She'd hoped to get dressed, climb down the fire escape with her bugout bag, and disappear. Like for good, out of the state this time.

Her hectic mind had her frozen in place and she stared at the slight line of blood rolling down the grout line. A groan coming from behind her snapped her attention back to her immediate problem.

Running wasn't an option now. Tony would know she was alive and he'd never stop looking for her. And when he found her, he would make her pay for every moment of the chase. For daring to leave him, even worse for tricking him. Tony didn't take humiliation well.

She'd made him look like a fool before in front of one of his drivers. Someone he saw as so far beneath him he never even learned his name. She'd corrected his pronunciation of scourge. Rachel doubted the driver had even heard, but that didn't matter to Tony.

He'd ripped her dress down right there in the back seat and put out his cigar on her breast, but not before ordering the driver, *"Hey you, make sure you're paying attention."*

After the sizzle had stopped, he was turned on and forced her face down on his dick while he traced the lines of the wing tattoo on her back with the fingertip blade he wore on his pinkie.

That wasn't the worst of the memory coming back either. Tears sprung to her eyes, and she dropped to the tiles and hugged her knees as she relived the rest.

She couldn't spit or swallow. Luckily, they had been close to home. He marched her into the house . . . breasts and burn exposed, small trickles of blood ran down her back and his cum choking her.

"If you vomit, you will lick it off the floor, so be a good girl and do as I tell you and I may allow you back in my good graces." His voice had been sickly sweet and cold at the same time.

Vin had been there when they entered. He always seemed to be around when Tony needed to humiliate her. *"Hey brother, let's see that big dick you're supposedly known for?"*

Rachel was remembering things slightly different this time as she raised her head and saw Vin's blacker than sin eyes fluttering as he shook his bald head in an attempt to clear the blow she'd dealt him.

That day she'd always recalled it as lust on Vin's face when he freed his tattooed dick, but now she wasn't so sure. It seemed for the first time in her memory, he hadn't wanted to obey his brother, but he did all the same. *Weak ass bastard.*

"Tony, what's going on?"

"Ah, brother of mine, you are about to experience the sweetest mouth God ever created." Tony pushed her to her knees in the marble entryway and guided her to Vin's feet. *"Now my sweet angel, suck, but don't swallow."*

The terror of that day coursed through her there on the bathroom floor above the garage. The memory transported her back in time. The humiliation had been all-encompassing. Even worse had been the realization that all Tony's threats to sell her to buddies in the sex trade were soon to be her reality.

Tony had already started stroking himself through his trousers at the thought of her sucking someone else's dick. That day, Rachel realized she had no choice.

She pled with just her eyes, but Tony was focused on her lips and Vin's dick anticipating when she would open her mouth full of his fucking cum and blow his brother.

It was meant to humiliate them both, Rachel realized in hindsight. She remembered looking up at Vin right before she leaned forward. His eyes left Tony and flew to the corner of her mouth where she was losing the battle to contain her own saliva mixed with the vilest thing imaginable at the time.

For a moment she saw confusion and mortification cross his face, but that turned to disgust. Before she could degrade herself further, Vin backhanded her, and she fell to the marble. The action caused her to spit the contents of her mouth on his shoes.

"What the hell, man? I do not want your fucking jizz on my dick."

Tony had laughed so hard she'd thought he'd piss his pants.

Another groan from the radiator pulled her attention away from the past for a moment. Vin's eyes were fluttering at a different rate now and staying open just a bit longer each time. Still unfocused but she felt he could see into her soul.

That night Tony had scolded Vin about damaging his property, but there had barely even been a drop of blood. Her hand flew to her cheek as if she could still feel the slight sting. It hadn't hurt much either, now that she had a clearer head to think about it.

Vin's punishments never did.

A lot of things seemed different in hindsight but the more credence she gave them, the more convinced she was she suffered from a mental defect. What kind of person suffers abuse and then justifies it, excuses it, and finds a man like that attractive?

As much as she hated Vin, she cared for him too and she hated herself for that. Somehow, she'd managed to convince herself he wasn't as bad as he'd seemed at the time.

Vin's actions that day had gotten him saddled with her for three nights.

Tony tossed his hands up. "I'm bored of her anyway. You're up, Vin. No clothes, no food, and no touching. I've got a hot number waiting in my room. I'll send for that when I'm done." Tony spat on the floor and strode up the stairs. "Remember, no touching my property. You didn't want my generous offer, so you get nothing."

Vin gripped her arm, pulled her to her feet, and dragged her to his room. That was one of Tony's favorite games. Make her sleep naked in Vin's rooms. He got off on it somehow.

Once behind closed doors, Vin's face always got harder somehow. Colder, even when his words were gentle . . . for him anyway.

"Sit. So, what did you do to bait him this time, Little One?" He got peroxide and bandages and tended her wounds as he always did, even when he caused them.

Rachel didn't answer.

As bad as that night had been, one of the worst, it was also her salvation. That was the night she decided to leave and began planning. She knew she wouldn't survive much longer. She would be sold into the sex trade or Tony would kill her. Either way, she knew she had to get out.

Rachel had to save herself, and she had done just that . . . until tonight.

She dashed away her tears with her fist and stared at the face of the only person who'd seemingly cared for her and loathed her at the same time. There had been so many times she'd thought there had been something redeemable in Vin and he would help her escape.

Yet every time that thought buoyed her hopes, he did something like backhand her in disgust to sink it.

His eyes were opened now without drooping lids but still unfocused. She rose and walked to him on shaky legs.

Rachel bent down and looked deep into his eyes. *Silly girl, he was never going to be your hero . . . but wasn't he somewhat my hero?*

She hadn't realized how close she'd gotten to his tied hands until he touched her cheek. It almost felt like a caress. *Stop it.* She jerked away so fast she ended up right back on her ass.

"Rachel? How? I mean . . . thank God you're alive."

"How isn't important. But now that you've found me, I'm a dead woman. You killed me, for good this time."

Rachel was horrified at her mixed feelings toward Vin, but what did any of that matter now in the grand scheme of things?

If she killed him and ran, Tony would figure it out and come looking for her. If she didn't kill him, well, he'd take her back and the consequences would be worse than death. Her only choice would be to convince Vin to lie for her.

Make up a story about how one of Tony's enemies faked her death and kidnapped her. They could go back, Vin a hero and her a poor victim. Her punishment was sure to be less that way.

She looked at Vin and wondered if he would give her one thing before she went back to hell. No matter how he chose to take her back, she would ask.

Rachel had only ever been with two men, the one she lost her virginity to and Tony. One was a humiliating grope fest, which turned out to be a painful joke and Tony was just plain cruel.

She wondered what it would be like if cruelty and pain weren't a part of sex. She knew Vin wasn't a good guy but she was convinced he didn't have the same perversions as Tony. Besides, she'd felt his gentle touch when he tended her wounds. Or his soft caresses once he was deep asleep and cuddled her in the middle of the night.

Those were the only times in the last ten years she felt anything close to affection from another person.

If nothing else, Vin was a man. She'd noticed his physical reaction to her once or twice. While he may not have any emotional attachment, he did enjoy the sight of her as a woman and that would have to be enough.

A bit of bile rose in her throat as she over analyzed how she'd just relived one of the most humiliating sexual experiences of her life and was now thinking of touching the man who'd witnessed it . . . who'd been disgusted by it.

But this was her only chance to know non-abusive sex before going back to a living hell. One she planned to take her own life to escape as soon as Tony's guard was down enough for her to do so. So yeah, she had to try to have a normal, whatever the hell that was, experience.

That blow to the head must've rattled his brain good because he'd just looked into the eyes of a dead woman, they weren't cold and colorless. He'd touched her warm, pinked cheeks.

Vin's brain was playing catch-up, but it was more like a cassette unraveling in the player. Sounds were weird, colors were off, and there was Rachel, looking like a cancer patient. Only silvery gray stubble covered her head like freaking GI Jane style or some shit.

His heart dropped to his gut at the thought that she was sick. Apparently, she was the Tabitha Annabelle said had cancer.

Vin's semi-focused eyes raked her form. She sat unmoving on the tile where she'd fallen after he touched her. She was at least twenty pounds lighter than the last time he saw her. That had only been a week ago, how could that be?

Sick or not, that wasn't possible. Confusion, hurt, elation, relief, anger, and emotions Vin couldn't even recognize were warring for superiority. Waiting for one to win would be futile, so he just started with what came out first and they could work their way from there.

"Explain?"

"You'll have to be more specific than that. Explain what, the meaning of life? The chemical composition of fertilizer? The—"

"STOP!" Yelling was a bad idea. His vision blurred and his temple pounded. When he went to grab his head, Vin realized she had tied him with a knot he could easily break out of. A slight twist and a little muscle and he could touch her in a way he was never allowed to before. Not that she would allow him to do that. He was the asshole who hit her more than once, her jailer, her abuser by proxy.

A ghost of a smile touched his lips. He'd do it all over again if given the choice. Many times his abuse saved her from a fate so much worse. Vin hated touching her harshly, but if he hadn't taken the initiative, the shit Tony would've done to her would've been disgusting and harsh would seem like a vacation.

His brother was unstable as fuck, but Vin knew his games and how to play them to save Rachel as much torture as possible. Of course, she didn't know that, and neither did Tony, thank God.

Had either one figured it out, she wouldn't be scrambling to her feet right now, and he damn sure wouldn't be tied to a radiator.

Nope, Vin would be in prison, and Rachel would be on her back in some filthy house in Singapore or somewhere, or if she were lucky, dead.

Judging by the terror on her delicate face and the sheer fear in her emerald eyes, Vin decided to stay put and not mention how easily he could free himself.

"Don't play dumb, Little One, not with me. Explain . . . now."

His words were a command, but his head had drained all the fire from his voice.

Vin watched her pace the small space like a trapped predator and prey at the same time. The trapped prey was a posture he was used to in her, but the predator part was new. The Rachel in front of him was different somehow. He liked the backbone she had displayed but he didn't like her fear and turning in on herself.

"You're giving me a fucking headache trying to focus, can you be still already?" His voice had lost all fire.

It was her, Rachel somehow managed to rob him of his past and soothe a part no one else could.

Vin felt he was a slightly better person in her presence. One he could almost imagine might have a semi-normal life if someone like her loved him . . . almost. There was nothing remotely normal ahead for him, he knew that, but he was a little delirious after that blow and finding her alive, so he allowed himself to indulge a bit.

Indulgence wasn't delusion though. There was nothing for them and right now he had to shake off any fanciful musings he had and focus. She was alive . . . for now, but how in the fuck could he keep her that way.

"Rachel?"

She abruptly halted her pacing and spun to face him with flames in her eyes. "Why the fuck would I tell you?" The blaze extinguished as quickly as it had flared. Her posture told the truth about it.

"That's not important. It was a long shot, one that worked like a dream until you couldn't leave well enough alone. Why are you here anyway, Vin?"

"You know why I'm here. Tony doesn't leave anything to chance. I was simply clearing everyone at *your* service."

Rachel began to pace again. Vin could practically hear the wheels turning in her mind.

"Since my life is forfeit, at least tell me how you made the connection with Tabitha, she didn't go to the service."

It was chance, but Vin wasn't sure she'd believe that. Had Tony sent anyone else, she would be safe.

"I didn't, I mean I did, but not like you think." Vin had no intention of revealing his feelings to her . . . ever, but she was smart and he knew that his next statement could have her connecting dots. He steeled himself for the disgust that would surely follow.

"I trailed Eunice from the service. Clearing her was a formality. She's old as fuck and no threat to Tony, even if you'd spilled your guts to her. I was pretty much done, ready to head back when I saw the vase."

Vin watched her spine stiffen and her eyes go impossibly wide. There was a slight smirk hidden under her self-chastisement. He'd puzzle that shit out later.

"I'd know your work anywhere. The desk lady said Eunice placed it there and Tabitha had made it. I followed the breadcrumbs Annabelle gave me. I expected to find someone who meant enough to you that you gifted your first sculpture to her. When I got here, I was sure of it. I had thought you'd taught her, obviously . . ." Vin trailed off as things started clicking into place.

While other things left more questions. "How do you know Eunice, by the way? Just curious, I swear she is safe." Vin added the last when her green eyes turned to hard emerald stones. Cold and sharp.

Right before she burst into a fit of laughter. He didn't care that she was losing her fucking mind, Vin wanted to know what she meant to her and not for Tony. Then something else struck him.

"Wait, how in the fuck did you drop twenty pounds in a week?"

Apparently, his ignorance amused her because she was practically pissing her pants laughing. Vin jerked his arms against the rough rope. The radiator groaned under the assault and that grabbed her attention.

"Sorry." She dashed at her tears of mirth. "It's just, I so rarely get to laugh about anything. I really did have the perfect plan if not for that fucking vase. How you remembered . . . that is beyond me." Thank God she didn't seem to assign any weight to him remembering.

Vin watched as her whole body language changed. She slumped and shuffled across the small bathroom. "Oh dear, I seem to have forgotten where I was headed."

Vin was gobsmacked. Rachel was Eunice . . . and Tabitha. He realized how much she had grown, right under his nose and he'd missed it.

When Rachel straightened her body and looked him in the eye, he almost didn't recognize her. "The twenty pounds was a lot harder than aging sixty years. I lost the weight over the last few months, but I padded my clothes so no one could tell. I told Tony I was being treated for a sexually transmitted infection, of course, he wanted no part of that. Then I stayed as low key as I could so as not to piss him off or he'd send me to you. I was positive you'd have noticed." Lower he heard, "You noticed everything."

That felt like the fucking lie of the century. He hadn't realized she'd finally had enough and saved herself.

And I just fucked it all up for her.

"And the illness?"

"An assumption that worked in my favor."

Vin breathed a sigh of relief.

CHAPTER 7

Rachel was more confused than ever. Vin being in her bathroom, *Tabby's* bathroom, meant an end to her freedom. But somehow, she had made peace with that. *Yep, I've finally given up.*

Mostly because she was tired. Tired of . . . everything, even life itself. There was something freeing in no longer trying to survive, accepting your mortality. Statistically, she should be dead already, she was on borrowed time as it was.

Why not experience what she could, maybe help Vin out with Tony as a bonus. As shitty as Vin had been, his actions had always helped her over the years regardless of intent—

A thought smacked her so hard she physically staggered, maybe, just maybe.

"Vin, do you remember that day in the foyer?"

His eyes darkened and she knew she didn't need to elaborate, he remembered. The disgust was as clear on his tanned face as it had been that day.

"Why bring that up, Rachel? That was months ago." The subject appeared to resonate with him as much as it did her. Another realization crashed into her. Vin used her name as a means of distance.

Vin called her Little One most of the time and as twisted as it sounded, even to her, it was a borderline term of endearment. He'd only ever called her Rachel in front of Tony or when he seemed separated from the situation.

All this time she'd thought she'd had Vin figured out, but she'd misjudged him. Took him at face value, the one he presented anyway.

Now, she couldn't help but dig deeper. Maybe it was curiosity that drove her, or perhaps it was to justify her own feelings toward him, either way, she would have answers. *Whether I like them or not remains to be seen.*

"Because, I'm curious, why would you turn down a free blowjob?"

His voice boomed in the small room, echoing off the tile and scaring the shit out of her.

"WHY? Because I would never humiliate you like that . . . like *him*." His answer was exactly what she needed or wanted to hear. This man wasn't all blood and violence, regardless of what she'd seen. Rachel felt herself soften even more toward him, and she viewed Vin through different lenses.

"Don't go all gooey-eyed, Rachel, the humiliation wasn't only meant for you. No fucking way in hell would I let him chump me like that." His words held a sharp edge, but his eyes betrayed him ever so slightly. Even the whispered words that followed couldn't hide the truth. He cared about her on some level. *"Like I'd ever stick my dick into a mouth full of his cum."*

Rachel shuddered at the reminder. Rubbing her arms couldn't rid her of the goosebumps that sprang up. She gagged at the memory and rushed to the toilet, but nothing happened.

Still, she rose and found the sink, loading her toothbrush with way more toothpaste than one person needed. Rachel scrubbed her teeth aggressively. It was something she did at least five times a day.

When she spun back around to Vin, he looked like he was on the verge of apologizing, but that never happened either. It wasn't in his nature.

Covering her lack of confidence, she took a knowing stance. Her arms crossed her body while she leaned back against the sink. She imagined she looked like she had the world by the short and curlies when in reality, she felt small and exposed.

"What about all those wounds you tended when Tony ordered my suffering? Or all the times you asked to discipline me, and you were more gentle than he would have ever dreamed of being or the nights you held me close and spoke sleepy words of fondness. What about—"

"ENOUGH! There are more pressing matters than rehashing the past. Tony will expect a report tonight, and if I say all's clear, I'll need to make lockdown at the compound."

"I have a proposal, one more time for you to play the hero, but this time to Tony not to me."

"I'm not a fucking hero." It was more growl than speech while his eyes held the truth of his words. He wasn't a hero, not like people expected anyway, but he had been *her* hero, even if he couldn't accept it. It was obvious now, he held at least a modicum of affection for her, even if she overestimated how much.

"Fine, poor choice of words. What if I had a way for you to save face with your brother, would you do it?"

The look that followed felt downright physical. It was as if he were taking inventory of her whole person. Every line, every curve.

"We're pretty much fucked, but I'm listening."

"I'll go back with you, I have a cover story all worked out, I only ask that you—"

"YOU WANT TO GO BACK TO THAT MONSTER?"

His shout confused her. No, she didn't *want* to go back, but she *had* to go back. Didn't he see that?

"Vin, you're not stupid, hell, you're one of the shrewdest people I know. We both see how this ends. I can never run far enough or fast enough to get away from him. Once you return . . ."

Rachel turned away so he wouldn't see her tears. *I can't convince Vin to make love to me if I'm crying.*

She heard the sound of scraping metal on tile and felt a presence behind her a split second before she was grabbed and spun around to face a very angry Vin.

"You honestly think I would take you back to him?" Vin seemed . . . hurt and his voice raspy and demanding. *That's new.* If she were confused before, it was a million times worse now.

He'd just proclaimed he wasn't a hero, but now seemed upset she thought he would do the expectedly non-heroic thing and take her back.

Vin's hands released their fierce grip on her biceps and traveled to her face. His eye contact was uncomfortably intense. It was as if he couldn't control his hands as they began to wander and his eyes traced the movement.

She trembled with such intensity she heard her own teeth clack together. *This is what I wanted, right?* Why did it feel so good and so terrifying all wrapped together? Maybe his touch meant something else entirely, something she didn't comprehend.

Rachel was well acquainted with what a cruel touch felt like, looked like. Vin's hands were slightly rough but in a non-threatening way . . . at least as far as pain went.

What little she knew of caring touch had come from him when she needed tending, and it didn't feel like that either. That had always been gentle but laced with pity.

Other touches she'd only read about in books she hid from everyone or the occasional television show she'd watched. It had to be one of those.

Vin's warm tanned hand brushed across her shaved head then they both landed on her shoulders and traveled down to her hands.

When Vin laced their fingers together for a brief moment before they moved to her narrow hips, something inside her melted away.

It was fear, one she hadn't realized she'd been gripping onto. Fear that Vin's hands would turn the way Tony's had in the beginning. Setting her up with sweet touches only to turn sour. Tony had liked that so much, the confusion on her face warring with the pain. Once she stopped falling for it, Tony had moved on to more vicious ways to elicit her reaction.

"Where are you?" Vin dropped his hands and stepped back. His onyx eyes betrayed him; he knew exactly where she was.

With one hand on his hip, he raked the other across his bald head. Scrubbing his scalp as if he had hair. Rachel felt the need to fix this, get back under the spell that the previous moment had held, but it was broken.

"Vin, I . . ." What could she say? She was damaged, ruined even. She could now see Vin was too, just not as irreparable as her.

He turned to the door as if he meant to leave but instead punched it. Wood splintered and Rachel yelped.

"That fucker well and truly did it. When you were dead, it was one thing, but to have you live and never be able to even touch you without bringing you to a dark place. FUCK THAT BASTARD."

He punched the door again, but his voice held only defeat. "You've finally won, Tony. You managed to rip everything away."

Rachel felt like she was being tossed about in a tornado. Her brain hurt just trying to make sense of everything.

"Vin," she spoke as gently as she could muster with her trembling voice. "I don't understand. I thought—"

CHAPTER 8

The thump of his forehead as he dropped it to the door cut off her words. He hated that he'd scared her, it wasn't his intention. But ever since he'd come to being tied to the radiator, his life had been completely torn apart.

Vin was not a man who knew love, at least not as normal people did, but he knew Rachel. He wanted to protect her from every single thing in the world, even himself. Causing her pain, hurt him on a damn near physical level.

Vin wanted to look at her face every day and feed on her smiles. Her light kept his darkness from being an all-encompassing pitch black. The darkness was never gone, not even she could do that, but it made it more of a dark gray for a few inches around her.

That's why he loved to keep her close . . . touching him was best. When she'd died, he was sentenced to a blackness that no light could cut through. Every single glimmer was snuffed before it had a chance to shine.

To find her alive was just . . . he didn't have the words for it. But Tony, fucking Tony, he'd planted the terror and pain so deep inside her that finding Rachel alive was tainted by the fact he couldn't touch her without dampening her light.

Vin wasn't sure he could face her or stomach the pain that swam in her emerald eyes, so he spoke to the door. All traces of his earlier anger had been washed away by Rachel. "Did you ever wonder why he always sent you to me but with strict instructions of no touching?"

"I don't know. Some sort of punishment in his mind, I guess."

Vin spun from the door, almost losing his balance in the process. Not because of his earlier blow either, it was *her*, she kept him off-kilter. Rachel had almost been upon him, her delicate hand reaching out as if she'd meant to stroke his back.

Their eyes clashed, black and green met violently and nothing else moved. Her arm still suspended and she held her breath . . . he did too.

Stepping into her touch was like nothing he'd ever experienced. This was the first time she'd simply touched him for the sake of touching him. That's how it felt anyway.

Their intense eye contact was broken when her lashes fanned down on her flushed cheeks. He groaned when he realized she was savoring the contact. Vin allowed his lids to fall and enjoy the sensation coursing through his body, flowing from her touch.

The last thing he wanted to do was break the spell, but he had confessions. Things he wasn't sure how she would react to and things that could destroy this very feeling.

"It was punishment, Little One. Torture. But it wasn't directed at you. My brother was punishing me. He knew I cared for you and being the sadistic bastard he is, found ways to punish me through you. I am so sorry, if I could take all that shit back I would, but I can't."

Vin didn't know how he could hide his joy at the fact she still breathed and throw Tony off, but he would, damn it. Even if he had to sacrifice an innocent person to his brother, he would not let him know she lived.

While the rest of his sins, the ones she didn't know anyway, were cued up and ready to go, that would be one he would keep from her. He owed her many truths, but that reality would serve no purpose for her.

Vin cried out at the loss of her touch until those caring hands landed on his cheeks. He burrowed into it, wishing the moment could last forever and they could live their entire existences within it. But that was not how life worked . . . not how he worked.

"You wouldn't have even popped up on his radar if it weren't for—"

"Shush," she urged him. "If I learned anything over the last years, it is that you are not responsible for anyone else, especially not a batshit crazy wannabe with a God complex."

Before he could allow himself to believe her words, he stepped out of her reach. It was physically painful to do so but he did it anyway.

"No, you don't understand. I saw you first and I wanted to talk to you and that's what condemned you to ten years of hell. If that wasn't enough, half the shit he did to you, he did it to hurt me. You were just the means. Collateral damage. Tony's real goal has always and will always be to make me pay for even being born."

Vin chanced a glance in Rachel's direction and could see the protest bubbling in her eyes.

"It's true, Rachel, like I told you, I'm not a fucking hero. Everything since the day you laid eyes on him has been my fault."

She rushed forward and fiercely embraced him. He could no sooner push her away than he could stop breathing. Vin bit the inside of his cheek to keep the rest of his confessions in his throat. He wanted to tell her that he never meant to hurt her, but punishing her was a choice he made to spare her? Would she even believe such a thing?

"Oh, brother of mine, if you go easy on her, rest assured I will not. What I do to her will make your worst nightmare look like rainbows and unicorns. Do you understand? If I tell you to punish the cunt, she better be punished."

A shudder crawled up his spine at the memory. How could he expect her to forgive him for laying hands on her no matter the reason?

Besides, I can't tell her that shit or she really will think I'm a hero and expect words and acts of love. Things I can never give her.

"Heroes never realize what they really are. So much seems clear to me now. I don't need you to confirm the things you did, Vin, I already know." The breath her words produced penetrated his thin tee shirt and feathered across his skin. They knocked gently at his chest and begged entrance.

Could he open his heart like she seemed to want? Vin wasn't sure he could do that, but he would care for her to the depth he was capable and protect her from all harm even if it killed him.

He would trade his freedom and his soul to free her and know she was safe for the rest of her long life . . . if that's what Rachel felt was love then he could give her that.

But how could he accomplish such a feat? The answer was a boulder that sat heavy in his gut. *Tony has to die.* The trick was lying to Rachel about it. Vin would be damned if she would have to live with having any part in taking a life, even one as corrupted as Tony's.

Vin lived with that shit every single hour of every fucking day and he wouldn't wish that on anyone, especially the woman in his arms.

Holding her quieted the voices and the demons and his past. He took the silence to think about their predicament. Her body felt so good, so right in his arms that other things were now keeping his mind from working.

Vin tried to put a little distance between them before he embarrassed himself by asking for something he didn't deserve, but Rachel held him tight.

Up on her tiptoes, she found his lips with hers. Vin froze. They were warm and insistent, but still, he was stone. Rachel pulled her face back enough to look into his eyes. Hers were soft and inviting, begging for every secret he had to tell, like a priest in a confessional.

Vin physically shook off the sensation. He couldn't . . . wouldn't tell her how he'd killed his own father. While they stood no actual chance as a couple, not in the real world anyway, he couldn't bear to see what her eyes would project then.

"You know, a kiss works better when it's shared."

Her words rocked him back on his heels. He assumed she was just caught in a moment, but it seemed she'd wanted to kiss him on purpose. "Why would you want to kiss me?"

The look which crossed her face brought a small tilt to his lips. Her hands left his body and landed on her hips. Her attitude was new to him and he kind of liked it. "Correct me if I'm wrong, but kissing usually happens when people make love, at least in books and movies."

His eyes must have betrayed him because her attitude dropped and her confidence fled. "Sorry, fuck . . . when you—"

CHAPTER 9

Rachel's words died on her lips as Vin consumed them. The kiss was rough at first, not wholly unlike the only ones she'd experienced. Yet, his hands were gentle, holding her face with tender regard rather than commands.

A tremble she couldn't control shook her entire being as her back pressed into the bathroom wall. Vin had her trapped and again there was a war waging within.

The sensations he was wringing from her with his tongue in her mouth and the grinding of his body against hers was sublime.

But . . .

The feelings being ripped from her by the memory of being trapped against one wall or another was shouting at her with deafening clarity. *RUN. FIGHT.*

"Shit," Vin cursed and left her personal space so abruptly she almost fell to the cracked tile.

"Rachel . . ." His large hands scrubbed down his face as he began to pace. "I'm sorry . . . I didn't think."

Vin's voice filled the room. "FUUUUCK!" His hands were now fists, clenched close to his thighs. He strode around the small space like a fighter pacing the octagon, gearing up for his opponent.

"Vin?" Her voice was weaker than she liked. It made her feel small and insignificant to cower, especially to him.

"No." His conviction took her aback. "Do not apologize. I can hear it in your voice. You owe no words of sorrow, not to me, especially not me. I . . . I just don't know if I can be what you want, what you deserve."

Vin was back to pacing. He spoke, but it seemed he was talking to himself and not her. "Hell, you had ten years of being treated that way, you damn sure don't need it from a man like me too. Not when you finally have a choice."

The words were still falling from his mouth. Sad and angry and . . . it tore at her soul to hear him like that. *It's not you,* she'd wanted to shout but somehow she'd become mute.

With a deep breath and shaky legs, Rachel stepped into his path, causing him to halt. He made to go around her, but she stopped him with a spur of the moment idea. She crossed her arms over her hips and grabbed the hem of her tank, swiftly ripping it over her head, voluntarily exposing herself.

She wore no bra, she didn't need one, so she stood for a half a second in only loose-fitting sweats she'd hastily donned earlier when she'd heard the noise below.

Vin was like stone, unmoving. If it weren't for his widened pupils and intensity swirling in his onyx eyes, she'd swear he actually was.

Before she lost her nerve, she bent and removed her sweats. When she was upright once again, she met his eyes and refused to look away. Even when his eyes tracked up and down her body, lingering on her breasts and between her legs, she stared straight into his soul.

One step, two, and she was just a whisper from touching him. She dropped her gaze enough to find the opening of his pants. With shaky fingers, she slid the zipper down. The noise seemed impossibly loud and echoed off the porcelain and tile surrounding them.

Vin's hands halted hers and their eyes locked. Rachel's were hot with anticipation of caresses she'd never known but still craved. Vin's were warming but remained cold from some internal struggle she didn't understand but could practically reach out and touch.

When the two warring temperatures collided, it created an atmosphere that was electric with a coming storm. An atmosphere of . . . them. It was theirs and theirs alone.

Rachel knew that moment would change everything. For better or worse remained to be seen but the change would happen.

For the first time in what seemed like forever, Rachel trusted her instincts and put herself into Vin's keeping.

This could be the best thing I've ever done or the second worst, only time will tell.

Rachel wasn't a fool, there was only one way out of the situation she'd gotten herself into years ago and that was death. Hers or Tony's, but death was the only answer. She would go back and protect Vin the way he'd so clearly done for her for far too long and death would come for her, but not this afternoon. This afternoon was hers.

Whatever answer Vin was looking for in her eyes, he must've found because he released her hands only to cradle her face gently and kiss her the way they did in the movies.

His lips were in control but not controlling. Gentle wasn't the right word but they were . . . caring? His fingers massaged the back of her neck and he tilted her head for a perfect angle. She was drunk off his lips alone and thought, *this is how it's supposed to be*. Vin continued to drink from her lips, nibbling the lower one every so often as she undid the button and slid his pants and boxers down his thick thighs.

A wiggle assisted her as he toed off his shoes. Before she could reach for his shirt, he released her face and lips.

"I'll do my best to be gentle but it's not my first nature. If you can't handle that, I understand completely but you need to tell me now. Like I said, I'm nobody's hero so I'll not stop later. You need to be sure, Little One."

In answer, she reached for his shirt and slowly peeled it over his head and took in his body. He may have sported a bald head, but his body was anything but.

Unbidden, she found herself taking inventory and comparing him to Tony. Considering he was the only man she'd ever truly seen all of in the light, it wasn't a conscious decision.

Where Tony was lean, Vin was bulky. Tony, smooth and waxed, Vin furred and natural.

Dark hair was sprinkled liberally across his chest. Her hands had a mind of their own and before she could assert control over it, her fingers were buried in the silky thatch between his pecs. Vin groaned and his blacker than sin eyes shuttered.

Rachel's eyes followed the dark trail that arrowed south and took in her first real glimpse of his cock. It stood proud and thicker than any she'd ever seen with black hair surrounding the base. She remembered seeing a few inches of it before but she'd tried to forget that day.

This was different, she wanted to look at it today, even the thought of taking him in her mouth didn't disgust her.

Today is different.

With uncertainty, she allowed her hand to follow her gaze. It took the same path her eyes had until it arrived at the same destination.

Without real experience, Rachel felt lost. She had only ever done what she'd been instructed to do, touch where she was told and when. But this was Vin.

Rachel chanced a glance at his face, his eyes were open and watching her intently. The emotion that danced in them gave her confidence. She'd never touched a man who looked at her as Vin did. Was it love? She wasn't sure, but whatever it was, it was safe and that was all that mattered to her.

Rachel gripped the shaft and slid toward the head. Her fingers never met her thumb, but her grip was firm and Vin groaned. She repeated her action and elicited another rumble from him, and he thrust into her hand.

Rachel broke eye contact to look down between them. The tattoo ran the length of his cock and up onto his body.

Readjusting her grip so her thumb faced her, she added her other hand below the first and began pumping up in earnest. Even with both hands wrapped around him, there was still a good inch of shaft left exposed below the darkened head.

Doing the only thing she could think to do, she leaned forward and spit on the head, taking up the wetness with her hands. Vin's shout rang out and his hands dropped to the top of her shoulders.

"Don't stop now, Little One, grip me tighter . . ." She did as he bid and tightened her grip, twisting clockwise as her hands rose and countered as they retreated.

"Fuck me . . . faster, Little One, faster." Vin fucked her hands as she jackhammered her efforts. Vin embraced her and their bodies were pressed so tightly together she could barely continue her ministrations.

He came with an animalistic sound that shocked her. Her hands and their bodies were sticky but she continued a slow pump until he commanded her to stop with what sounded like a small laugh.

VERLENE LANDON

CHAPTER 10

Vin held Rachel tight. He was still reeling from a hand job. *A fucking hand job.*

How that could send him into a tailspin he didn't fucking know, but it did. God, when she'd spit, it turned him into an animal. It was so primal.

The little wisp of a woman who'd been through hell at the hands of his brother and himself opened up to him.

She could've just as easily turned in on herself with the shit she'd been through but somehow she managed to take her life back. And she'd just gifted him something huge.

Being inside her was all he could think about even though he'd just emptied his balls in her hands. Vin scooped her up and ignored her yelp of surprise.

He turned for the door and stood in front of it waiting for her to open it. When she figured out what he wanted, she attempted to turn the knob. Her hand couldn't get purchase on the worn smooth orb. For the first time in a long time, Vin laughed. Rachel joined him. He found himself wondering if that was what normal people did. Laugh about jizz on a doorknob?

Finally, her hands found enough grip to turn the knob and open the door. Wasting no time, Vin dropped her to the tiny bed-like thing in the corner of the room. It was more of a rickety fold-out, but it would work.

Vin allowed himself just a second to take all of her in. She was perfect, he was even grooving the thinner, no hair look. What he didn't groove were the small scars that marred her body. They were a part of her, so they were beautiful all the same, but each one Tony needed to answer for.

With the slightest of touches, his fingertip gently kissed the one at her breast. One he'd seen fresh and angry. One he'd treated and was dismayed to see scarred more than he'd hoped.

Rachel's hand landed on top of his, pressing it against the slightly puckered skin. "Don't, please. I want to feel nothing but pleasure and affection. No pity, not now, not like this."

A slight nod and he clenched his jaw against his inclination to inventory every mark he'd treated, every one he'd caused . . . every one he could've prevented if he weren't such a fucking coward when it came to Tony.

With a deep breath, he pulled out of that swirling vortex trying to bring him under and focused on the place he most wanted to be, the place he meant to taste first. He stepped to the end of the bed and dropped to his knees on the worn carpet.

Vin grabbed her ankles and pulled her toward his waiting mouth. He released them to the top of his shoulders and wrapped his arms around her thighs. With his fingers, he spread her beautiful pussy wide and had his long awaited taste of her.

That moment made the other good moments in his life pale in comparison and eradicated the bad. Taking lives, hurting people, wishing his brother dead, none of those held any sway over him with his tongue buried inside her.

She tasted of silence. The silence of his past and his deeds. The moment was oppressively mute except for Rachel's moans of pleasure.

Vin used his nose on her swollen clit without removing his tongue from her. When she grabbed his ears and steered him like a bike, his cock went impossibly hard for someone who'd just shot a load not five minutes ago.

With a tinge of regret, he replaced his tongue with his fingers and suckled her clit. She screamed his name and rocketed into pleasure when he nibbled at her. Without slowing his fingers, he studied her face. The shock, the confusion, the pleasure, all glittering in the purest green he'd ever seen.

"Shit." It was a barely breathed word. He had a feeling, but he hadn't known for sure. That was the first time she'd had a mouth on her pussy, that was clear and it was also the first time someone had ever pleasured her.

Now he had a new mission in life. Protecting her wouldn't be enough, he had to pull that kind of pleasure from her body regularly. If that was to be his penance, God really was on his side for once.

Vin slid up her body smoothly. "That was . . ." Her breathless confession trailed off. Vin found his lips devouring hers.

"Oh, Little One, if you think that was good, grab your ankles and hold on tight." Vin tilted his hips and entered her in one stroke, committing her expression to memory.

The resistance her body offered was ecstasy. When she reached down and grabbed her ankles as he'd suggested, he lost his battle for a gentle and controlled fuck.

Furiously pumping his hips, Vin chased that sharp-edged moment where nothing existed except pleasure.

In mere minutes, that moment was on top of him. His eyes still locked on hers, he licked her tit. Sucking the nipple deep into his mouth earned him his name on her perfect lips.

Needing to speed her up and give her another moment of pleasure, he pinched her clit and then circled it in time with his thrusting hips. He felt her body start to tighten and he forgot how to breathe. Nothing or no one could stop his orgasm from crashing into him with a force he'd never known. "FUCK."

His shout seemed to go on forever, as did his pleasure. Spurt after spurt, he just kept coming. Finally when his balls were empty and his cock not very impressive, he realized she was still writhing on the edge.

Shit, I fucking came without her.

He worked his thumb against her body with furious intent and felt her finish. It wasn't perfectly time mutual pleasure, but how often did that happen anyway?

Rachel's gripping body prevented him from slipping free, but he was okay with that. With other women, he'd pull out before he nutted and was dressed before he'd gone soft.

He wasn't finding it wholly unpleasant to still be inside her body. The panic didn't overtake him at the thought of enjoying the afterglow as it always had.

When Rachel's body relaxed, he slipped free. Balancing on the tiny surface, he took her in his arms, resting his head on her chest. He'd never done that before, not even with her as she slept in his bed.

She returned his embrace fiercer than he'd expected. Vin felt loved, listening to her heartbeat and wrapped in her arms. He curled his entire six feet and two inches around her tiny body like a child and just existed in the moment. No thoughts of what was to come or what had been.

Just a normal man in someone's arms. Vin allowed the illusion to take over and he laid there listening to her heart and breath. The stickiness of what they'd just shared started to dry uncomfortably and he figured if it broke through his fantasy then she was damn sure miserable.

With great effort and a heavy sigh, he extracted himself from her embrace. Before he made it to the bathroom, a sad sound grabbed his attention. *What the fuck is—*

"Oh, shit." Vin walked to the chest and opened it. The little black fucker leaped out and rubbed his legs as if they were best friends. "Stupid fucker," Vin muttered and went to the bathroom to clean up. Once he was de-jizzed he grabbed another cloth and wet it for Rachel.

Vin wanted nothing more than to ignore his phone vibrating like crazy in the pocket of his pants on the floor, but he couldn't.

Tony's suspicion was probably already up. It always was if he missed any communication from him, even by seconds.

Grabbing the offensive device, he saw the ass-ton of missed calls and texts. Calling back would be folly so he texted instead.

> Vin: Nothing here of note, one more thing to check and I'm headed back.

Before he could drop it with his clothes, it pinged again.

> Tony: A little bird told me the bitch had an old friend and that the old friend led to a young one. Did you find the young one? If she is anything to look at, I want her. I heard she's sickly and dying, but she still has a pussy and maybe a few months. Find her, bring her, and we can share.

The text disgusted him, but more than that, it terrified him. Any hope of convincing Tony there was nothing to be found had flown out the window. Now he had to come back with a *young one* or he had to run. Neither of those would work, so killing Tony was now for sure the only answer.

Vin only had one problem, how to protect Rachel while he went to handle Tony. He couldn't leave her now, not since it was obvious Tony knew about her. He must've had Luke running double checks, or he would've known exactly where to find her.

Small blessings.

CHAPTER 11

Rachel was half out of it as Vin was cleaning her. It was a gentlemanly thing to do, although she wouldn't tell him that. Vin would deny even the possibility that he had a gentlemanly bone in his body.

Once her hands were clean, she reached for his cheek and opened her eyes to him. What a difference a few minutes can make. She could practically see the wraiths flying in swirls all around him. His eyes were more haunted than she'd remembered them being.

What could've happened between here and the sink? All traces of the warmth she'd felt when they were joined was gone. Sure he was doing something caring, but it was if by mechanics.

His sharp face was void of the earlier emotion she saw in every angle. His eyes were again fathomless black depths holding nothing tender. Pain and nothingness were all she could find in them.

Rachel realized he had dressed, even had his shoes on. *He already has one foot out of the door.* Only one thing could've disrupted their tiny taste of paradise.

"Tony?" She hated the quiver of her voice as she spoke a name she wished she could forget. It tasted like blood and death on her lips.

Vin chucked the cloth across the room. It landed with a wet plop that gave her chills. It couldn't be that bad, they could run, or she could, and Vin could report back to reassure Tony and join her tomorrow. They could figure things out while they hid. Well, the only thing to figure out was how to rid them of Tony since he'd refused to take her back.

Vin stood and scrubbed his hands over the top of his head. His posture told her it was worse than she suspected.

"He wants Tabitha brought to him."

The soft words sent ice shards through her veins, slicing and freezing her from the inside. Scrambling off the bed, she dressed in record time.

Rachel grabbed her bugout bag. "Then we need to go now. We can figure it out later, but if we leav—"

Vin grabbed Rachel and spun her to face him. The old Vin mask was down. His eyes were distant and flat.

"If we run now, we will be running forever." A flicker of the Vin from earlier, the Vin she shared her body with, was present. He cupped her cheek. "We will spend our lives looking over our shoulders and that's no way to live."

Rachel dropped to her ass to the bed. *We're fucked. Yep, someone has to die.*

"I have to go back, but I need you to be safe." Vin reached for her bag then and grasped her arm. They were halfway down the stairs while Vin was explaining where she would go before he finally heard her voice.

"VIN . . . stop." She wrenched her arm free. Before she could even speak another syllable, Vin looked at her with frustration and barely contained aggravation. He tossed her bag to the garage floor below and turned on her in the enclosed narrow stairway.

His size pressing into the walls and invading her space made her feel claustrophobic. Vin's anger sucked all the available oxygen from the air.

"Damn it, Little One, we don't have time for this. Get your ass in gear or I will toss you over my shoulder." Vin seemed to realize his posturing and stopped. His face softened and defeat was etched across his features. "I can't do this if I don't know you're safe. I need you in this world, Rachel. Drawing breath and bringing light even if I can't be there to see it."

What is he . . .

"What do you mean not be there?" She slapped both hands down on his chest and shoved. He tripped backward down the remaining stairs but managed to stay upright.

Rachel followed him down in a flurry of righteous anger. Poking him in the chest and looking up into his face, she felt small but mighty cloaked in her outrage.

"You were going to send me away and not even pretend you would join me? Do I mean so little to you that you could just . . . out of sight, out of mind. Is that it?"

Her ire was sky high now. Granted, she expected their actions to be a *last meal* kind of thing, but somehow she felt more of a connection that she'd expected. Plus, the things he'd said . . . done.

Fuck me, I'm a fool. He told me he wasn't a fucking hero, but I wouldn't listen. Lesson learned.

Rachel knew the thought that sprang to her mind was wrong, even more so to express it, but she had never played by the rules, even when it cost her dearly.

"You're no better than T—"

"Don't finish that sentence, Rachel. I mean it, don't even fucking think it."

Rachel yelped when Vin punched the wall. He didn't even bother shaking off the drywall before he grabbed the back of her neck and kissed her brutally.

Their teeth crashed together and he made a sound almost like a cry before he pulled back to stare into her eyes. That black storm was swirling there again. His voice was soft but fierce.

"I am nothing like that bastard, Little One. I hit walls when I'm pissed, he hits people. He wants you so he can bring you, or Tabitha, nothing but unimaginable pain, I want to bring you nothing but unending pleasure."

Vin dropped his hand and his head. "He would turn you over to a sadistic prick to save his own skin if that were an option, I would send you away forever and take the punishment meant for you instead."

Vin turned from her then, looking older than before. Picking up her bag, he clapped his hands against it.

"I don't think that's an option now, if I'm being honest. It sounds like he already has people out scouting for Tabitha or soon will have. Checking up on me is right behind that. I wanted you safe and nowhere near that bastard, but the safest place for you is by my side."

He tossed the bag to the old tool chest in the corner, narrowly missing her new sculpture. One she realized held so much meaning now. The eye was Vin's and the apocalyptic chaos reflected in it was coming up, the tear was all hers.

It was time for Rachel to face her demons, or rather demon. She was terrified and shaking with the thought of seeing Tony, but she needed to do this. Closing this chapter would free a piece of her that she left trapped with him.

A piece that she wanted, no, needed to reclaim. Rachel chanced a glance at Vin. He would never see her the same once she killed his brother. Her wholeness meant more than any man did, even Vin.

"I can see the wheels turning in your head, Vin. It's okay, really. I need to face him to be whole again."

Wrapping her arms around him, she let the spicy smell of his cologne comfort her. She let go of the idea of him being her hero and realized she had to be her own. If Vin wanted to be one too, that was fine, but she needed to do this, save herself one more time.

"Please, understand. It's not you putting me in danger or protecting me. It's about me facing down the last ten years of torture and reclaiming the woman I was always meant to be."

Vin's embrace tightened almost painfully and he kissed her head.

CHAPTER 12

Vin didn't know what to do or say, she impressed the fuck out of him. So brave even though she was trembling. His need to keep her far from Tony was pressing in on him with the force of a tractor-trailer, but he knew he would lose her for sure if he denied her.

Every cell in his body was screaming at him to fuck it and pack her off to a safe house anyway. Going against his desires and putting someone's needs ahead of his was foreign.

Vin had lived, existed is a more apt description, for his own self-preservation. Doing Tony's bidding so he could remain free-ish.

At first, Tony had guilted him with his dad's death, but as time went on, that guilt shrank. The man was a total dick and deserved to die, hell, their dad had beaten the fuck out of him relentlessly. When he started on Tony, Vin reacted.

Vin finally decided the deed of taking Tony's dad from him was paid. By that time, he'd already committed crimes for Tony, which he used to keep Vin in line, and so on. He knew that cycle would continue until they tossed him in a hole, dead and cold.

Many times he'd decided to pack up and just disappear, if Tony turned him in, he would turn state's evidence and implicate Tony, but he was a chickenshit and never did.

At first, it was because he just couldn't bring himself to turn on his brother, a man who blamed him for taking their father's life. At some point, Tony ceased being his brother and basically became their father, just worse.

When that truth slapped him in the face, he was on his way out for real, finally, but that was when Tony brought Rachel through the door. From that day on, he never packed a bag again.

Now he held her in his arms and she was free of that fucking monster, but she had to go back. Who was he to tell her she couldn't face him down? He couldn't protect her from one monster only to expose her to another.

Vin held her that much tighter at the thought. At least he'd experienced paradise first.

"You're an incredible woman, Rachel. You're right, you deserve to face him. So, let's do this." Vin left the *together* implied.

It sounded lame, but Vin had nothing else. He wanted to beg her not to go, he wanted to take her back upstairs and sink into her welcoming body and fuck her into a stupor until she relented.

Rachel was too strong for that, he could see that now. He'd always thought her stronger than most, but in this light, he could see how terribly he'd underestimated her. She'd survived a decade because she was strong as fuck. Then she devised a pretty sound plan and freed herself. She never waited for some mythical fucking knight to ride in and save her, nope, she was simply biding her time to save herself.

God, he fucking wanted to use the L-word. Not just proclaim it to her, but to himself. He wanted to feel it, but he wasn't capable of traditional love. However, what he felt for her was as close as he could come and it was deeper than anything regular people could feel.

He would die for her if he had to. Most men would for their women, but how many would kill for them? Oh, they all proclaimed it in their tuxes in front of men who claimed to speak for God, but how many actually would?

Vin knew beyond a shadow of a fucking doubt he would, sooner rather than later at that.

Vin gripped her cheeks and stared straight into her light. He dropped his lips to hers in a telling kiss. Letting his lips speak the words of his heart even when his vocabulary couldn't.

Slowly and with single-minded focus, he backed her into the nearest wall. Releasing her face, his hands went to her waistband and pulled her sweats down and over one shoe.

"Wrap your legs around my waist," he commanded as he undid his own pants and freed his cock.

Rachel obeyed without hesitation. As soon as she did, Vin entered her body. No foreplay, no sweet words or petting, nothing.

He had to pump his hips a few times—exerting more control than he felt, just to get balls deep, but when their hips met, he groaned in ecstasy.

"Fuck, you're perfect." Vin was selfish at first. *Which is why she's so perfect for me.* His need to feel her around him, consuming him, had taken over all other thoughts.

She moaned his name and he remembered he was not trying to just enjoy one last time with her, he wanted her to feel what he felt, he wanted her to feel loved in the best way he could.

Vin needed her to know the depth of what he felt for her and if she labeled it love, that was fine by him.

Dipping his head, he tasted her perky pink nipple. He wanted to order her to grab her tits and serve them to him, but he wasn't sure how she would react to that. Instead, he nibbled the other and listened to her moan louder.

If time had been on their side, Vin had a menu of shit he wanted to explore with her. Shit, that would probably be firsts for her just like earlier, but that was not meant to be.

Vin wanted to get his message across, but he needed to speed up the delivery. Releasing her tit, he looked around the darkened garage and spied a low workbench. *Perfect.*

Walking her the short distance while balanced on his cock was interesting. He turned and sat with her on his lap. The change in position damn near did him in. When she repositioned her knees at his hips on the bench beside him, he gritted his teeth against the pleasure.

Vin set the pace with his hands at her hips. Rachel laced her fingers behind his neck and picked up the pace he'd set which freed his hands for other pursuits.

Grabbing both tits, he squeezed and fell upon her chest. Reading her body, he realized exactly what she liked and he kept that shit up.

One hand left her tit to venture down to where she rode him. Her body was so sensitive to his touch and he played her clit with precision. Pinching and rubbing just so until she came screaming his name.

Her pussy rippled around his dick and he followed helplessly. Vin dropped his head to her chest in an effort to return his breathing back to normal and held her tight.

"I'll kill for you, Little One." He prayed to a God—who'd forsaken him long ago—that she knew how much that meant and it would be enough for her.

She kissed the top of his head and he could feel her smile. "I'd kill for you too, Vin."

Those were the best words she could have uttered.

CHAPTER 13

The ride to Tony's was a blur. It seemed like a lifetime and a flash all at the same time. It was taking forever and her brain had way too much time to turn itself inside out. When they pulled through the gate, she could've sworn they only just left the garage.

Vin was strapped with an obvious handgun at his back. She assumed multiple hidden weapons too, as he'd always been. Rachel had a small butterfly knife and that was it.

Her hastily devised plan, the one she solidified on the longest-shortest trip of her life, was to allow Tony to take her away from Vin. Once they were away, she knew Tony's routine, he'd make her strip, then and only then would punishment come.

That meant her window was small, damn near microscopic. She'd have to shed her shoes and then her top. When she reached for the waistband of her pants, that would be her only moment.

Tony would be sitting in his chair in the "fun" room with a lit cigar, watching her strip and perusing the various implements of pain he kept on the table next to him.

If luck were on her side, she'd grab the knife, flip it open, take two steps and drive it into his throat.

Of course, there was a chance he would dangle the cigar from his lips so he could caress one of his tools. If that were the case, there was a chance he would lift one in defense and she'd be dead too, but a small price to pay.

Vin would find them after the fact, but then he could move where he wanted and start over. Maybe have the family he deserved instead of a psychotic brother.

The thought of him with another woman was a lump in her throat, but he would be happy and away from Tony . . . and so would she.

Many times she'd thought of death, hell, living with Tony it was a looming presence. Either he would kill her or she would take her own life. Every time he came close he told her, *"Oh, no Sweet Rachel, you will not get away from me that easily."*

And every time she thought of ending it herself, she chickened out. No matter how bad shit got, Rachel always held out hope that there would be something worth living for.

Sometimes she found it to be something as little as tacos, others, as big as thinking it was better her than someone else. If she were gone, the thought of Tony finding another naïve girl to take her place terrified her.

The sound of the engine ceased and she looked up at the looming building through the window. *Man, it sure looks so different now than it did ten years ago.* She knew the horrors that hid behind the ornate doors and pristine white columns. No one wants to see behind the curtain.

Vin was silent and stony. His chest barely rising and falling with his breath. It was up to her to take the next step. Vin obviously didn't want to be the one to take her inside.

"You ready? We should probably go in before Tony wonders why it's taking so long. The gate would have called ahead."

When he turned to face her, he was white knuckling the steering wheel. Something lurked in his eyes she'd never witnessed before. "Is there anything I can say to convince you to get in the driver's seat right now and crash out of here and drive until you run out of gas?"

Rachel reached over and broke his death grip, taking both his hands in hers. "No. Whatever happens, happens. Just know that no matter what that is; you gave me something no one else ever had. And that made everything else worth it."

Tears sprung to her eyes unbidden. She released his hands to dash them away before they fell. She'd be damned if Tony would see her weak ever again.

Vin nodded once and exited the car. Rachel waiting until he came around and let her out, on the chance Tony was watching. If she failed to kill him, maybe it would at least look good for Vin that way . . . maybe.

"Remember, Little One, I'm not a fucking hero." His voice was sad, for a moment she wondered if he wanted to be. Rachel touched the knife at her back for reassurance as Vin opened the door.

A sense of déjà vu overtook her. The last time the house had been this deserted was when Tony brought her home and laid out the rules of her new life.

It was her first night living there and he wanted to set the precedence. *"It's time you learn exactly what I expect from you, sweet Rachel."*

In the beginning, Tony had been dashing and gentlemanly with just a hint of danger. After a few dates, his abuses started, small at first, and then he graduated to using his fists. By the time he brought her here, she was already conditioned. That night though, she learned she had grossly underestimated how much worse it could get.

A shudder surfed the length of her body. Tony thought Vin would return victorious with Tabitha and he would have a new toy to terrorize until she'd had enough too.

Rachel knew she wasn't the first, but God, how she would damn sure be the last.

"Ah, my brother returns, and I hear he brought me a gift." The voice floated to her from deeper in the house. It was like a bad movie scene. Tony was seated in an obnoxious leather chair turned away from them. The top of his head and the cigar between his fingers were all that was visible.

He'd yet to turn around. It was his attempt to strike fear in the new toy. *You have the element of surprise,* she screamed in her head. *Rush him, slit his throat and be done with it.* Nothing or no one in jail could be as scary as he'd been all those years. Yet, her feet stayed rooted in place.

It wasn't until he started to turn, she finally exerted control over her own muscles and started to move.

Just a few more steps and they would both be free of the living nightmare of a man.

Everything moved and sounded like she were underwater. She heard her name being called, followed by a slow and drawn out *no*. It was Vin, somehow her stalled brain recognized that.

The eyes that had tormented her for ten long years were finally looking at her. Looking but not seeing. She watched in slow motion as they went from curious to shock to recognition to rage.

The things cycling through Tony's eyes terrified her. She saw her past and her future, her pain and sorrow . . . and her end.

It was just two or three seconds of her life, but it drew out forever.

Raising the knife, she struck him, but her scream, a sound she didn't even realize she had made, gave him time to shift. Her knife sunk into his shoulder. Rachel felt it halt when it hit bone. Her strike wasn't strong enough to drive through it.

That was the moment real time came back to her. It sped up to what would be normal and the underwater dream feeling vanished.

Tony grabbed for her and spun her around. He wrenched her hand and the knife free, taking it from her in the process.

She was locked in his grasp. His voice was in her ear and her own knife at her throat.

This is it, my end. Tony's pride wouldn't allow for her to live long. She would rather he do her in now instead of later. All she could do now was save Vin since she'd failed so miserably at saving herself.

CHAPTER 14

The word *no* died in his throat as Tony grabbed Rachel and had a knife at her throat. He knew his brother well enough to know he would end her as easily as breathing if the urge struck him.

Vin had been so shocked, he hadn't even reached for his gun. The terror in Rachel's eyes ripped his beating heart from his chest, then a strange calmness flowed into the green orbs.

She mouthed, *I love you,* and it was his salvation and his condemnation. He shook his head, knowing she was about to do something stupid, but she was no longer really seeing him, she was looking right through him.

"Damn you, you fucking asshole. I can't believe you brought me back here. I can't believe I ever thought you were different. I hope you rot in hell."

Tony laughed and it was not a pleasant sound. Tony amused meant bad shit would follow.

"Oh, brother, looks like you pissed off the little lady. How does it feel to love someone and know she despises you? Know that the fun I'll have with her, she'll blame you for. I couldn't have done it better if I had planned it myself."

Confusion swirled all around him, clouding . . . everything. One minute she said she loved him and the next she was damning him. His brain knew it was part of some last-minute plan to save him and sacrifice herself, but it still stung a hell of a lot worse than it should have.

Faked or not, the fire behind her words drove them into his heart. He felt every syllable, regardless of intent.

Vin was lost in the eddy of emotions before he realized he was wasting precious time. He could feel real things later, if he were lucky. For now, he would use her hate and pain to play the part she'd cast him.

But she would pay later, *if she still cares for me after the night is over, that is*. He had said no to her plan but now he had no choice. Tony's voice cut through the haze that had wrapped around him.

"And you, sweet Rachel, how did you manage to fly the coop so effortlessly? No matter, I don't care, you won't get another chance, so the how doesn't matter.

Since we've already had the funeral, there is only one thing left to do." Vin watched as Tony drew a drop of her blood with the tip of the knife, licking it off in some sick display of power.

Tony slid his other hand around her body, stroking her stomach and grabbing her breast. "I have to say, I am liking the non-blubber version of you. Maybe I'll fuck you just once more before I kill you. Oh, or better yet, fuck you *while* I kill you."

Rachel whimpered and Vin bristled. "Tony, enough."

Tony pointed the knife at him. "You don't tell me when enough is enough, little brother." He spat the words like an insult. Vin realized he had been drinking, and drunk Tony made mistakes. Mistakes like taking the knife from Rachel's throat. If only he'd already had his gun out.

"Besides," Tony whispered and turned his attention to Rachel. "She is *my* toy, not yours, *never* yours. Even if I let her go right this second, she wouldn't run to you, dear brother." It was the first time Tony seemed to actually think since they'd walked in.

"That begs a very good question, why? Why bring her back to me when you wanted her for your own? You could've run away with her and had a happily ever after, so why didn't you?"

Vin reached for his gun but didn't draw it yet. Tony still deemed him a non-threat. The second he pulled it, that would change and Rachel would be in deeper danger than she was already,

"Ah, I know why, she wouldn't have you, would she?" Tony was amused at the thought, it was clear. "Just like your mother who dropped you at our doorstep and my father who despised every inch of you. Poor little unwanted Vincent, even I only kept you around because it served me."

Vin wasn't an idiot, he knew his brother bore no love for him, but hearing it was still a harsh dose of reality.

Tony licked Rachel's cheek and left a pink streak of saliva-diluted blood. It was a sick display, but he couldn't look away.

It was then Tony turned his eyes toward him again. He could see it wasn't just alcohol but some touch of madness that was burning in his brother.

For the second time, Tony laughed. "Look at you, standing there loyal as fuck. You brought me the woman you love and for what, a pat on the back? You're so pathetic. You don't know how many times over the years I thought you would rise up and take my seat the way I did Dad's, but you never did. You stayed loyal as the mutt you are."

The way he did Dad's? But Vin had killed their father, it was the sole reason he joined his brother in the first place.

"What do you mean, I killed our father to protect you and you had no choice but to take over, Lord knows I wasn't about to."

Again, for a moment, Tony left an opening he could've exploited had he drawn his weapon already, but he was reeling from the things his brother was saying. Something was wrong, and he needed to know what it was now.

He chanced a glance at Rachel and she seemed as confused as him, but safe for the moment. Besides, the more Tony talked, the sloppier he got, so all Vin needed to do was let him talk and then taunt him enough to drop his guard and he could take him out.

"You're as stupid as Dad always said you were. Do you think he ever laid a hand on me the way he did you? Fuck no, I was his heir, he'd never hurt me. He had you to take his anger out on."

"But I saw him, I saw—"

"You saw what I wanted you to see." Tony's anger was rising. "Dad was defending himself from me when you came riding into my rescue just as I knew you would. He was half dead before you dealt those killer blows.

Even so, the stab I gave him to his gut would've done him in no matter what."

It seemed to take forever for the words to resonate in his head. "You tricked me into killing our father?" The horror in his voice was reflected in green eyes.

"*Believing.* I tricked you into *believing* you killed our father. He was still alive when you left the room as I told you to. I choked the life out of him and watched it drain from his eyes. It was a magical moment."

"You're even sicker than I thought you were." It was a horrified whisper from Rachel, but it earned her a vicious hit and she fell to the ground on the edge of consciousness.

Vin wanted to go to her but that was the wrong move to make. He was still reeling from the fact his whole life had been built on a lie. What could he have been if not for that? Who could he have been?

Tony placed the knife on the side table and smoothed his suit as if he'd just stood from the dinner table. He pulled Rachel to her feet and kissed her cheek.

He sat down with her on his lap and retrieved the knife.

Damn me to hell, he'd let her go, but I stood here like a fucking idiot. Vin would never forgive himself for that missed opportunity.

Drawing the knife up and down Rachel's chest without cutting her, Tony seemed lost in his own head.

He really did believe Vin was unconditionally loyal and why wouldn't he. Vin had never done anything to prove himself otherwise.

Vin cursed himself yet again for the missed opportunity to take Tony out, but his brain wasn't firing on all cylinders with the truth bomb Tony had dropped.

Vin was more right than he'd ever been when he'd told Rachel he was no hero. No truer words had even been spoken.

Vin needed to refocus and get Tony to drop his guard again. He would have to say things he hoped she'd forgive him for one day.

I may not be a hero, Little One, but I can damn sure try this once.

CHAPTER 15

Rachel's heart was broken in two for Vin. To hear his greatest source of pain was a lie rocked him back. She could see the shift in him, the way his entire posture changed. Rachel felt it to her core.

Tony was in a state of madness. She'd known this side of him, glimpsed it ever so briefly over the years, but never this prolonged. Maybe he'd finally snapped. If that were the case, there was no telling what he was capable of.

One thing she knew for sure, if he took her out of this room, she wouldn't live to see the morning and God help her if she did. Her brain was working overtime trying to think of a weapon or anything she could use. If nothing else, she would fight him until he slit her throat.

Rachel would *not* dance that dance again. Tony didn't seem to suspect Vin of betraying him and that was enough for her. She was ready to die. Opening her mouth to start the end game with Tony, she was cut off by Vin's emotionally roughened voice.

"Oh, *brother*," he said the word with anything but affection. "Guess what? I had her . . . more than once. She practically begged me to fuck her. To rid herself of your taint. Of course, I leaped at the chance to stick it to you, by well, sticking it to her."

Rachel could barely believe her ears. Vin was talking about them as if it was a revenge fuck. *Could it have been?* He did remind her he was not a hero as they stepped into the house. *Oh my God, you idiot. You never could pick a man. Now you picked one even sicker than Tony, just in a different way.*

She tried not to listen to her inner voice. She wanted nothing more than to believe in Vin, but it was getting increasingly harder. Why hadn't he taken a shot at Tony? Why hadn't he done . . . something? *Because he was using you*, she heard in her head. *Using you to get revenge on his brother.*

"No!" Tony shouted aloud as she screamed the same in her head. The knife dug into her left breast. She felt the warm stickiness of blood soaking into her tank, but she didn't dare make a sound.

If she did, Tony might realize what he was doing and back off. Or he'd drive it deeper. She was torn between wanting him to end it and wanting to free herself and survive.

"Yes, brother, I had her more than once. By the time I was balls deep the first time, she was so primed for this" —Vin grabbed his crotch— "she was screaming my name in seconds."

Vin turned his gaze to her for the first time and winked. "Isn't that right, Little One?"

Tony was practically vibrating with rage beneath her, the knife leaving her breast to point at Vin.

"NO!"

"Yes, then I fucked her up against a wall. She said she'd never felt anything like it before."

Again, his gaze shifted to her. She felt as if he were trying to communicate with her but she wasn't sure how or what.

"Oh yeah, you love it, don't you, love *me*? Remember what I told you?" She remembered many things he'd told her, which one was she supposed to recall right now.

Tony wondered too because he brought the knife to her throat. "What did he tell you?"

"He told me he was no one's fucking hero."

Tony barked a laugh. "Ain't that the goddamn truth."

"I mean what I told you while I was still inside you, pumping you full of my cum."

Tony leaped up so fast she ended up on her ass. He was charging Vin. The underwater feeling returned.

That you will kill for me.

"Nooooo." The last thing she wanted for Vin was to have to end his own brother, but she was too late. Vin pulled his hand from behind his back. The steel of his gun glowed in the dim light.

The flash was bright and blinding, the sound ringing off the marble. Tony stopped in his tracks almost comically. Looked down as the knife clattered to the floor and then dropped like a stone to the ornate inlaid medallion.

Rachel just sat there, staring at the blood gathering on the marble tile and seeping out like the evil it was.

Pulling her eyes from Tony, she noticed Vin hadn't moved but was staring straight at her. His gun was still raised with a wisp of smoke rising up. His breathing was steady and deep.

Tony's second, Sam, came rushing into the room, weapon drawn. Without broadcasting his intent or turning his face from Rachel, he aimed the gun at Sam's head. "I'm in charge now, so I suggest you lower your weapon and give me the respect due."

"No," Rachel cried so softly, no one but her heard. *Told you*, that evil doubtful, and apparently smarter side of her hissed in her head.

Sam holstered his weapon. "Boss. You want me to clean up this mess for you then?"

"Yes, I do." Vin tucked his gun into his waistband and turned his attention to Tony. He reached down and took the ring from his finger. The ring was a symbol of station, the one worn only by the family boss.

Tony had been proud of the fact his dad had designed it when he built the *family*. They were really just a group of thugs who played at being mobsters and followed whoever was the most violent and took the *throne*.

Now she watched as Vin took it for himself. Was everything a lie? Had he been after the power all along? Everything she knew of Vin screamed no, but she had learned over the years to trust the evidence, not her heart.

Vin turned the ring over in the palm of his hand, studying it as if he'd never seen it before. "My first act as new boss is to deem Rachel untouchable. My last act as boss is to pass this to you."

Vin handed the ring to a stunned Sam. "Try not to lead like the dead cunt on the floor or you just might end up like him, because someone will damn sure take you out."

"Boss?"

"That would be you, Sam, not me." Vin was finally at her side, scooping her up into his arms.

It hit Rachel as he carried her out the door and deposited her into the car. He'd given up power and money for her. Not to mention, he really *had* killed for her.

When Vin fired up the engine and pulled away from the estate, she half expected the gate guard to stop them. Instead, he opened the towering wrought iron bars and gave them a half salute. They turned right and headed into the night.

"Where do we go now, Vin?"

He squeezed her thigh affectionately. "Anywhere we want to, we're free."

Free.

She twined her fingers with his at her thigh. The word sounded foreign, but it tasted so sweet.

"But we should probably grab your cat first."

"My cat? I don't . . . oh wait, you mean the stray I feed? Yeah, I doubt anyone else will feed him." After everything that had happened, Vin was worried about that stupid cat. The bottom fell out of her stomach.

"He'll need a name if we're going to keep him, and a bath." Rachel always wanted a cat, so the idea of keeping him felt . . . normal.

Vin chuckled before he spoke and it gave her goosebumps. "He already has a name, Little Fucker. As far as a bath, that'll be your department."

Rachel never would've imagined Vin curled up with a mangy cat, but the slight upturn of his lips flashed some pictures in her mind of just that.

"Vin?"

He turned toward her, taking his eyes from the dark road for just a second before turning back.

"Don't look at me like that, Little One. I told you before, I'm not a fucking hero, but I will kill for you."

He brought their hands to his lips and dropped a kiss on their fingers.

She would let him believe what he wanted to on that subject, because she knew better. *Have it your way, Mr. Not A Hero-Hero.*

"I don't need a hero if I have you."

Rachel dropped her head to his shoulder and let her eyes close. "And for the record, I love you too."

VERLENE LANDON

DEAR READER

Thank you for reading *Dangerous Curve Ahead.*

If you enjoyed this tale, please consider leaving a review and checking out my other books.

This book was previously released as Unexpected Hero.

PLAYLIST

This is the playlist the characters in this book "shared" with me as theirs. I listened to this music while writing the book to connect with them.

Listen on Spotify. https://smarturl.it/UHPlaylist

ACKNOWLEDGMENTS

I feel like I am repeating myself, but here goes.

I always have to shout out to my family first. Without their sacrifices, I would write nothing.

My team for this book, beta readers, ARC readers, edits, proofs, cover, etc. Every single one of you make a huge difference. One that, if you do it correctly, readers don't even notice.

As always, much love to the Vixens for just being awesome. Also, for your help naming Vin. Special nod to Amber and Angie for blurb help and moral support behind the scenes.

Thanks to wine for helping with this process, and a middle finger to gin for hindering it.

Everyone who supports me in any way, insert your name here, because you fucking rock!

ALSO BY VERLENE

ANTHOLOGIES

Vegas Strong
(Charity: The Code Green Campaign)

AUDIO

Ryder Hard

ORDERED SERIES
(best read in order)

DESERT PHANTOMS MC
*The Black Stetson *0.5*
Thunder *1*

IMAGINE INK
Indelible You *1*
Brand Me *2*
Irrevocably Mine *3*
Inevitably Yours *4*
Unmistakably Us *5*

STAND-ALONE & THEMED SERIES
(can be read in any order)

Exit the Friendzone
On the Road to Love

Second Chance Detour
On the Road to Love
Dangerous Curve Ahead
On the Road to Love
DIY Hearts
#Lovehack
*The Black Stetson
Bar Hop
Ryder Hard

The Black Stetson is 0.5 in the Desert Phantoms MC. It does NOT need to be read to start the series. It is the unofficial introduction to some of the members and the backstory of Bullseye.

ABOUT VERLENE

Verlene was born and raised in the south. Thanks to the military, she's traveled the US, but now calls Sin City home.

Self-proclaimed zombie apocalypse enthusiast, word porn peddler, human canvas, Manowarrior, serial grammar killer, rabid Bama fan, accidental dust bunny population specialist, and abuser of the word f*ck. She's thrown live grenades, survived the tear gas chamber and forced road marches, but still thinks writing and publishing are more brutal.

She's written countless stories and poems but didn't start publishing until 2015.

Verlene is on a mission to make naughty the new normal, one book at a time.

If you want to stay up to date on my latest releases & happenings...

- Subscribe to my newsletter. https://smarturl.it/VLNews
- Text Alerts – Text MyNextBBF to 88202
- Follow me on Amazon & Bookbub. Verlene Landon

If you like a healthy dose of naughty fun, giveaways, and sneak peeks at upcoming books before anyone else, join my Facebook reader group, Verlene's Vixens

- www.facebook.com/groups/VerleneLandon

I love to connect with readers, so feel free to use any of my links to find me online.
Verlene

- Facebook Page: Author Verlene Landon
- Facebook Profile: Verlene Landon
- Instagram: Verlene.Landon
- TikTok: Author_VerleneLandon
- Twitter: Verlene_Landon
- Signed Books & Merchandise: https://smarturl.it/ShopVerlene
- Email: Verlene.Landon@gmail.com